Short-h[...]
Mons[...]
in
Best Noise in the World

Z032277

Scholastic Children's Books
Scholastic Publications Ltd
7-9 Pratt Street, London NW1 0AE, UK

Scholastic Inc
730 Broadway, New York, NY 10003, USA

Scholastic Canada Ltd
123 Newkirk Road, Richmond Hill
Ontario, Canada L4C 3G5

Ashton Scholastic Pty Ltd
PO Box 579, Gosford, New South Wales
Australia

Ashton Scholastic Ltd
Private Bag 1, Penrose, Auckland
New Zealand

First published by Scholastic Publications Ltd, 1993
Copyright © Frank Rodgers, 1993

ISBN: 0 590 55314 3

Typeset by Rapid Reprographics, London

Printed and bound in Belgium by Proost Book Production.

10 9 8 7 6 5 4 3 2 1

Short-horned Monster
in
Best Noise in the World

Frank Rodgers

Hippo

Z 032277

$\dfrac{7195}{HJ}$

It was morning in the Monster Swamp.

The only sounds were the twittering of birds, the buzzing of insects...

5

and the CLATTER, BANG, BASH of the Monsters'
pots and pans as they made breakfast in their
mud-mounds.

The Monsters also sang loudly as they cooked.

LALALALOOO! BABABABOOOM! DEEDEEDEEDUM!
TRALA! They thought it was the
nicest sound in the world.

Everyone, that is, except Short-horned Monster.
He liked to sleep late and the other Monsters
always woke him up.

"Every morning the same," he said. "Worst
noise in the world!"

Short-horned Monster was a wonderful builder and suddenly he had a terrific idea.

He would build another mud-mound on top of his own and get away from the noise.

So that's what he did. But next morning in his first-floor bedroom he could still hear it.

CLATTER! BANG! BASH! LALALALOOO!
BABABABOOOM! DEEDEEDEEDUM! TRALA!

"Hmmm," he thought. "Have to live higher!"
He began to build another mud-mound.

This time the other Monsters gathered round.

"Who is this mud-mound for?" enquired
Greater-spotted Monster.
"Yes...who?" asked Lesser-spotted Monster.
"Me, that's who," replied Short-horned Monster.

"But you already have a double-decker mud-mound," said Hairy Monster. "High...*very*!"
"Ah," smiled Short-horned Monster, "but I'm going higher still."

"You mean," gasped the Monsters, "UP THE WAY? To the sky? Why?"

"To get away from CLATTER, BANG, BASH. LALALALOOO! BABABABOOM! DEEDEEDEEDUM! TRALA! every morning," said Short-horned Monster.

"Get away from the best noise in the world?"
The Monsters were amazed.

But Monsters always help each other so
everyone came and helped Short-horned
Monster to build more mud-mounds.

After the third
mud-mound they
built a fourth...

then a fifth...
then a sixth...

until they had
built twenty
mud-mounds
one on top
of the
other.

It was an incredible, dizzy monster mud-tower and it stretched right up to the clouds.

Ring-tailed Monster brought out a telescope so that everyone could see the top.

That night, Short-horned Monster had a
wonderful view of the moon and stars right
outside his window.

And next morning he slept as late as he wanted
because up in the clouds there was no noise
at all.

The other Monsters climbed up to visit.
"Just fill your ears with that silence," said Short-horned Monster proudly.

They listened.
"My ears are empty," said Hairy Monster.
"Exactly!" said Short-horned Monster.

But the Monsters didn't like the silence and emptiness all around them.

"Too creepy. We like the noises on the ground," they said. "The CLA…"

"I know! Don't tell me!" said Short-horned Monster. "The CLATTER, BANG, BASH. LALALAOOO! BABABABOOOM! DEEDEEDEEDUM! TRALA! Well I don't, so I'm staying here!"

"All right," said the Monsters. "Keep your horns on. Maybe you'll change your mind."
"Never," said Short-horned Monster.

But every morning when Short-horned Monster woke up to the silence of the clouds he felt sad. He missed all the noises down there, and was lonely but didn't like to say so.

Far below in the mud-mounds the Monsters knew this. They missed him too and thought of a plan to help him.

Up climbed Long-horned Monster and found Short-horned Monster twiddling his thumbs.

"Busy?" asked Long-horned Monster.
"Oh, got this and that to do, you know," replied Short-horned Monster airily.

"Too busy to build me a little outside toilet for my mud-mound?"
"Of course not," exclaimed Short-horned Monster, delighted to be asked.

Long-horned Monster looked round the mud-mound. "About this size?" he asked slyly.

Short-horned Monster got the idea.
"Have this one!" he exclaimed.

Long-horned Monster was the strongest of the
Monsters. He lifted up the mud-mound as if it
was a feather and carried it down to the ground.

Then Lesser-spotted Monster climbed up, taking
Long-horned Monster with her just in case.
"Could you build me a play-mound for Baby
Monster, please?" she asked. "About this size,"
she said, looking round.
"Have this one!" laughed Short-horned
Monster.

So Long-horned Monster whisked it on to his shoulder as if it was a sack of cottonwool and carried it to the ground.

After that all the Monsters came visiting and each one left with part of the mud-tower. Soon Short-horned Monster was back where he started.

The Monsters were delighted to have extra
mud-mounds and so pleased to get Short-horned
Monster back that they had a big party.

Next morning, Short-horned Monster was wakened by the sounds of the birds and insects and the noise of the Monsters making breakfast.

CLATTER! BANG! BASH! LALALALOOO!
BABABABOOOM! DEEDEEDEEDUM! TRALA!

Short-horned Monster smiled. "Ahhh," he
sighed. "The best noise in the world."